Quentin Blake

ANGELICA SPROCKET'S POCKETS

A Tom Maschler Book
Jonathan Cape • London

Angelica Sprocket lives next door.
Her overcoat has pockets galore.

There's a pocket
for mice,

and a pocket
for cheese

and a pocket for hankies
in case anyone feels that they're
going to sneeze.

There's a pocket for all kinds of umbrellas

for when it begins to rain.

And another one with
swimming costumes and towels

for when the sun
comes out again.

There's a pocket for ducks,
and a pocket
for boats

and a pocket with lovely straw hats

for GOATS.

And in case anyone is thinking
of dropping off to sleep,
there's a pocket for

motorhorns that go PAH-HEE-

HAR-HUR and BEEP-BEEP.

There's a pocket for skateboards
(just look at those
skaters!)

and another pocket for

ALLIGATORS.

There's a pocket for ice cream
and all kinds of nice things
to drink.

There's a pocket for
     saucepans and frying pans and buckets

and spoons and forks and cheesegraters and

the kitchen SINK.

There's a

pocket for an

ELEPHANT, green and pink,

and another pocket for…

WHAT DO
YOU THINK?

There's more and more
and more
and more.
Angelica Sprocket has pockets galore!

For l'équipe QB,
with love and thanks

ANGELICA SPROCKET'S POCKETS
A JONATHAN CAPE BOOK 978 0 224 08376 8

Published in Great Britain by Jonathan Cape,
an imprint of Random House Children's Books
A Random House Group Company

This edition published 2010

1 3 5 7 9 10 8 6 4 2

RANDOM HOUSE CHILDREN'S BOOKS
61–63 Uxbridge Road, London W5 5SA

www.kidsatrandomhouse.co.uk
www.rbooks.co.uk

Addresses for companies within The Random House Group Limited
can be found at: www.randomhouse.co.uk/offices.htm

THE RANDOM HOUSE GROUP Limited Reg. No. 954009

A CIP catalogue record for this book is available from the British Library.

Printed in China